Becci Murr

GRANDPA'S

CRACKER

WON'T
GO
BANG

For Emma Edmondson
with lots of love for being so supportive
of my authoring journey

ISBN:978-1-913944-24-7

Published by Llama House Children's Books

Grandpa had a cracker. It had spots of gold and green,

And Granny said it was the *finest* one she'd ever seen.

well-impressed

1

We pulled our crackers - **BANG! BANG! BANG!** - and festive treats flew out.

A plastic frog hit Uncle's face then landed in the sprouts....

Both Mum and Dad got marbles, Auntie's thimble broke a dish,

Then Granny had a piece of cellophane shaped like a fish....

Grandpa's hair before he grew too tall for it

But after hats were placed on heads and Christmas jokes were read,

Poor Grandpa held his **CRACKER** up and this is what he said....

3

My cracker isn't working, now I'm full of Christmas gloom,

I've tried my best to pull it, but it still won't go kaboom.

I really want some tweezers, or a plastic aeroplane,

A fake moustache that makes me look all **young and cool** again.

Oh, how I want a little helping hand from all the gang!

'Cause Christmas isn't merry when your cracker won't go bang.

When Grandpa
was all young and cool
(apparently)

5

Granny said, "Don't worry, dear, I'll eat this bowl of Brussels,

"For sprouts are full of vitamins and give you **bulging** muscles."

super-strong

She scoffed the stinky veggies then she tugged with all her might,

And pulled until her knuckles turned a snowy shade of white...

But as a little - PARP! - was heard and Granny's cheeks went red,

Poor Grandpa held his CRACKER up and this is what he said....

PARP!

super-pong

My cracker isn't working, now I'm full of Christmas gloom,

Your granny ate some **Brussels**, but it still won't go kaboom.

She thought that bowl of smelly sprouts would make her big and strong,

But all those leafy greens have done is make her bottom *pong*.

Oh, how I want a little helping hand from all the gang!

'Cause Christmas isn't merry when your cracker won't go bang.

Mother grabbed a string of scarlet tinsel from the tree,

"Let's pull it like a **TUG-OF-WAR**!" she shouted eagerly.

tinsel-tastic!

She wrapped it round the cracker, took the end and pulled it through,

But when she tugged the festive string, the tinsel snapped in two....

It flew up in the air and as it tangled overhead,

Poor Grandpa held his **CRACKER** up and this is what he said....

11

My cracker isn't working, now I'm full of Christmas gloom,

Your mother grabbed some tinsel, but it still won't go kaboom.

Her plan to use this sparkly string was positively silly,

And now my nose is itchy 'cause this tinsel's really **frilly**.

Oh, how I want a little helping hand from all the gang!

'Cause Christmas isn't merry when your cracker won't go bang.

13

Father heard the doorbell and he sped across the floor

To usher some bewildered *carol singers* through the door.

They formed a line, but suddenly their leader gave a shout:

"We're here to SING, not pull this old man's cracker!" he cried out....

But as the choir stopped pulling and began to sing instead,

Poor Grandpa held his cracker up and this is what he said....

15

16

My cracker isn't working, now I'm full of Christmas gloom,

Your father searched the doorstep, but it still won't go kaboom.

When carol singers come to call, you don't invite them in,

They'll make you **pull your lugholes off** to stop the awful din.

Oh, how I want a little helping hand from all the gang!

'Cause Christmas isn't merry when your cracker won't go bang.

Auntie left the table, saying, "Just leave this to me,"

Then came back with a donkey from the school nativity.

an ACTUAL donkey!

The creature chomped a turkey leg and scoffed the stuffing meat,

Then quickly **clamped its teeth** around my grandpa's festive treat.

The donkey tripped, its gnashers slipped, and as we watched with dread,

Poor Grandpa held his **CRACKER** up and this is what he said....

19

My cracker isn't working, now I'm full of Christmas gloom,

Your auntie **STOLE A DONKEY**, but it still won't go kaboom.

I love all kinds of animals, I'm just that sort of chap,

But eating lunch is tricky with a donkey on your lap.

Oh, how I want a little helping hand from all the gang!

'Cause Christmas isn't merry when your cracker won't go bang.

21

Uncle flung the window open wide without a word,

And then did something

absolutely,

utterly

ABSURD!

He took a carrot from a bowl,

He placed it on the ledge,

And through the open window....

23

Auntie's getting outta here!

My cracker isn't working, now I'm full of Christmas gloom,

Your uncle called these reindeer, but it still won't go kaboom.

They've trampled on my taters with a big old gravy-splash,

And no-one likes a **hairy spud** or hoof-prints in their mash.

Oh, how I want a little helping hand from all the gang!

'Cause Christmas isn't merry when your cracker won't go bang.

Everyone around me went completely **BARKING MAD!**

I watched as Granny poured a jug of gravy over Dad,

Then Uncle used the yule log like a tiny baseball bat,

As Mother put the turkey on her noggin like a hat....

And just as Auntie launched the stuffing balls across the room,

Poor Grandpa skidded on the mess

and something went....

stuffing balls
or reindeer
poop?

Poor Grandpa gasped, but as his face began to smile instead,

He spied a little fake moustache and this is what he said....

GRUMPY ELF

not a
caterpillar

31

I slipped and pulled my cracker, now there's no more Christmas gloom,

I slid on something yucky and my banger went kaboom.

This fake moustache is better than a plastic aeroplane,

And now your ancient grandpa looks all **young and cool** again,

Oh, how this grandpa loves to have a little 'tasche to wear!

But...

33

The hilarious series of gran-tastic catastrophes!

Becci Murray

GRANNY GOT A **sprout** STUCK UP HER SNEEZER

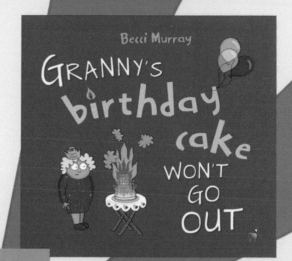

Becci Murray

GRANNY'S **birthday** cake WON'T GO OUT

Becci Murray

GRANNY DROPPED HER **chompers** DOWN THE TOILET

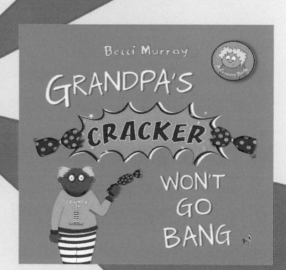

Becci Murray

GRANDPA'S **CRACKER** WON'T GO BANG

www.llamahousebooks.com

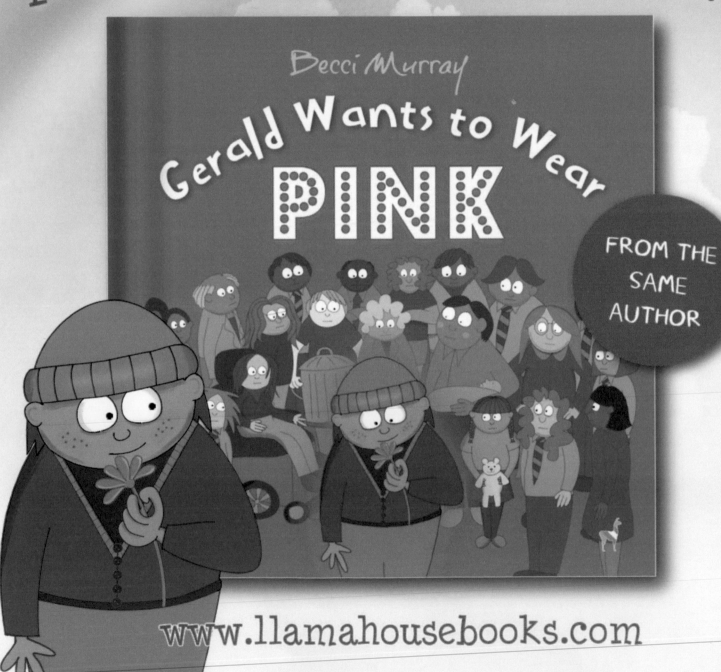

A fabulously fun rhyming read!

Becci Murray

Gerald Wants to Wear

PINK

FROM THE SAME AUTHOR

www.llamahousebooks.com

Becci Murray is a proudly independent author from the UK. She previously wrote for children's television and is the creator of the best-selling 'Granny' book series.

If you enjoyed Grandpa's Cracker Won't Go Bang, please consider leaving a review wherever you purchased the book to help other young readers discover the story.

www.llamahousebooks.com

Printed in Great Britain
by Amazon

11956645R00022